To Emma

Thanks to Gail Schwoebel

My Weirdest School #9: Miss Tracy Is Spacey!
Text copyright © 2017 by Dan Gutman
Illustrations copyright © 2017 by Jim Paillot

ISBN 978-0-06-242936-0 (pbk. bdg.)—ISBN 978-0-06-242937-7 (library bdg.)

Typography by Celeste Knudsen
17 18 19 20 21   CG/LSCH   10 9 8 7 6 5 4 3 2 1
❖
First Edition

Miss Tracy Is Spacey!

Dan Gutman

Pictures by
Jim Paillot

HARPER
An Imprint of HarperCollinsPublishers

Contents

Welcome, Miss Universe!

My name is A.J. and I hate putting on plays.

Plays are dumb. You have to learn a bunch of lines. You have to stand up in front of the whole school. Everybody's watching. If you make a mistake, everybody laughs. Ugh, I hate plays.

I had to be in a play this week. Here's what happened. Most days I take the bus to school. But sometimes my dad drops me off on his way to work. When we pulled into the drop-off line the other day, there was a big sign on the front lawn of Ella Mentry School. . . .

WELCOME, MISS UNIVERSE!

My dad slammed on the brakes.

"Sorry!" he said. "I was reading that sign."

"Who's Miss Universe?" I asked.

"Hmmm," Dad replied. "We'd better park the car and go inside to find out."

"Don't you have to go to work, Dad?" I asked.

"Your education is more important to me than work, A.J.," he replied.

We parked the car and went inside. There was another sign in the hallway. . . .

MISS UNIVERSE IS COMING

TO MR. COOPER'S CLASS!

That's my class! Dad and I walked a million hundred miles to the classroom. Dad walked really fast. It was like he was in a race or something. I guess he was in a hurry because he had to go to work.

When we got to Mr. Cooper's class, you'll never believe who was sitting in the back of the room.

Ryan's dad.

And Michael's dad.

And Alexia's dad.

And Andrea's dad.

And Emily's dad.

And Neil's dad.

All the dads were sitting in the back of the classroom! Even some dads of the kids in other classes were trying to get into the room. The place was crawling with dads!

Some of them had to stand because there weren't enough chairs.

That was weird. Usually our moms are the ones who come to school for assemblies and stuff.

I said hi to Mr. Cooper and put my backpack in my cubby. Then I went to my seat. That's when our principal, Mr. Klutz, came into the room. He has no hair at all. I mean none. His head looks like one of those mannequins in a store window.

"Is Miss Universe really going to be here?" one of the dads asked Mr. Klutz.

"Will we get to meet her?" asked another dad.

"Can we get our picture taken with Miss Universe?" asked a third dad.

"Gentlemen!" Mr. Klutz replied. "Please calm down and stop pushing and shoving. Miss Universe will be here any minute, and you can all get your pictures taken with her."

"Yay!" shouted all the dads.

The only one in the room who didn't look happy was our teacher, Mr. Cooper.

"I was going to do a math lesson this morning," he told Mr. Klutz.

"Miss Universe is only available for a short time," Mr. Klutz told him. "So you'll have to save that math lesson for another day."

Fine with me. I hate math.

Mr. Klutz went out in the hall. I turned

around and saw my dad fussing with his hair. That was weird. I never saw Dad fussing with his hair before. He hardly even has any hair to fuss with.

We had to wait a long time for Miss Universe. The dads in the back of the room all looked like they were on pins and needles. But they weren't. At least some of them were sitting on chairs. It would hurt to be on pins and needles. Finally Mr. Klutz came back in the room.

"I'm happy to report that Miss Universe is here!" he announced. "Boys and girls, I'd like to introduce the one . . . the only . . . Miss . . . Universe!"

All the dads pulled out their cell phones

and held them up so they could take pictures. And you'll never believe in a million
hundred years who came through the
door at that moment.

Nobody! You can't come through a door.
Doors are made of wood. But you'll never
believe who came through the door*way*.

It was Miss Universe, of course!*

She was a short lady with gray hair who
looked a lot like my grandmother. She
was wearing a big yellow hat with ten-
nis balls, Ping-Pong balls, and some other
balls hanging from it.

"Hi everybody!" Miss Universe said. "My
name is Miss Tracy. But you can call me

---

*Who else could it be?

8

Miss Universe, because I'm here to teach you about astronomy."

"Ohhhhhhh," the dads in the back of the room groaned.

Astronomy? What's that?

Andrea Young, this annoying girl with curly brown hair, had already looked it up on her smartphone. "Astronomy is the study of stars, planets, and outer space," she said.

All the dads stood up.

"Look at the time," one of them said. "I'm going to be late for work!"

"Me too!" a few of the other dads said.

"I have an important meeting!"

"I have a train to catch."

"So do I!"

All the dads started pushing and shoving to get out the doorway.

"Wait!" shouted Mr. Klutz. "Don't you

want to have your pictures taken with Miss Universe?"

"No time!"

"Sorry!"

"Gotta run!"

A minute later all the dads were gone. That was weird.

I guess they didn't want to meet Miss Universe after all.

Space Week

Mr. Klutz told us it was Space Week at Ella Mentry School. He said Miss Tracy is a retired scientist who spent her whole career studying astronomy.

"Are you a mad scientist?" I asked her.

"Well, sometimes I do get mad," Miss Tracy replied.

Oooh, she's a mad scientist! Mad scientists are cool. Miss Tracy will probably try to take over the world. That's what mad scientists do.

"Miss Tracy will be visiting our school for the next few days," Mr. Klutz told us. "I have to go to a meeting now, but I'll check back later to see how you're making out."

Ugh, gross! I'm not going to be making out with anybody!

Mr. Klutz left. Mr. Cooper went to the front of the class with Miss Tracy. He looked like he was still mad about missing his math lesson.

"What will you be teaching us?" Mr. Cooper asked as he passed out name tags so Miss Tracy would be able to call us by our names.

"We'll be learning about planets, stars, black holes, asteroids, meteors, and everything to do with outer space," she replied.* "But mainly, I want to show your students that astronomy can be fun. In a few days we'll be putting on a little play about astronomy for the school."

Oh no. A play. My worst nightmare.

"I love plays!" said Andrea. "My favorite play is *Annie*."

Ugh, Andrea said the *L* word.

"I hate plays," I said.

---

*Gee, something tells me there will be Uranus jokes in here.

14

"Oh, you just say you hate plays because I said I love them, Arlo," said Andrea, who calls me by my real name because she knows I don't like it. "You always say the opposite of me."

"I do not," I said.

"See?" said Andrea. "You did it again. I bet you secretly like plays, Arlo."

"I do not. Plays are boring."

"Oh, I promise you *this* one won't be boring!" said Miss Tracy. "Learning about the planets is fascinating."

The only thing I know about planets is that our old teacher, Mr. Granite, came from a different one. He was born on the planet Etinarg (which is "Granite" spelled backward). He came to Earth in a space-ship. But then one day another spaceship came, and the aliens took Mr. Granite back to Etinarg. We were all sad. That's when Mr. Cooper became our teacher. You can read all about it in a book called *Mr. Cooper Is Super!*

"Let's start by talking about the sun," said Miss Tracy. "The sun is big. So it's the center of attention. I need a volunteer. Who wants to be the sun?"

"I do!" we all shouted.

Andrea was waving her hand in the air like she was stranded on a desert island and trying to signal a plane.

"Okay, Andrea, you can be the sun,"

said Miss Tracy. "Come up to the front of the class."

"Boo!" said everybody but Andrea.

"Yay!" said Andrea as she ran up to the

front. "I should be the sun. My mom tells me that I'm really bright."

"How come *she* gets to be the sun?" I complained. "It's not fair!"

"I have an important job for you too, A.J.," Miss Tracy said. "I need you to be a planet."

Being a planet could be cool, I guess.

"Well, okay," I agreed.

"Great! Come up to the front, A.J.," said Miss Tracy. "What I need you to do is revolve around the sun."

"*Ooooo,*" Ryan said. "A.J.'s going to revolve around Andrea. They must be in *LOVE!*"

"When are you gonna get married?" asked Michael.

If those guys weren't my best friends, I would hate them.

"I don't want to revolve around Andrea!" I shouted.

"Okay, okay," said Miss Tracy. "A.J., sit down. Emily, would you like to be a planet?"

"Sure!" said Emily.

She might as well. She's always revolving around Andrea anyway.

"Great!" said Miss Tracy. "Andrea, you stand right here in the middle and don't move. Remember, you're the sun, the center of our solar system. Now, Emily, I'd like you to walk slowly around Andrea. You're planet Earth."

"I'm scared," said Emily, who's scared of everything.

"You'll be fine," Mr. Cooper told Emily. "There's nothing to be afraid of."

Emily started walking around Andrea.

"Good," said Miss Tracy. "Every time Emily makes one lap around Andrea, it's called an orbit. That's one year. It takes Earth 365 days to travel around the sun. So there are 365 days in a year."

Huh! I didn't know that's how they measured a year. I always thought the year ended when you ran out of days on the calendar and your parents had to buy a new one.

"Now, Emily, keep revolving around Andrea," said Miss Tracy, "and at the same time, I need you to turn around in circles."

Emily kept walking around Andrea and started turning around as she walked.

"While the Earth revolves around the sun, it also spins, or rotates," said Miss Tracy. "That's what causes night and day. Remember, Andrea is giving off a lot of light. When Emily is facing Andrea, it's daytime on that half of the Earth. When Emily is facing away from Andrea, it's nighttime."

Emily walked around Andrea and spun at the same time.

"Daytime . . . nighttime . . . daytime . . . nighttime," said Miss Tracy. "See?"

"I'm getting a little dizzy," Emily said.

"Is that why we see the sunrise and

21

sunset?" asked Neil, who we call the nude kid even though he wears clothes. "Because the Earth spins?"

"Yes!" said Miss Tracy. "Very good, Neil."

"Are we almost finished?" asked Emily.

"I was in a play where I had to sing a song about the sun," said Andrea. "The song went like this: Sunrise, sunset . . . sunrise, sunset. . . ."

It's so annoying when Andrea sings. Why can't a truck full of planets fall on her head?

"Can I stop now?" asked Emily.

"Keep spinning, Emily!" said Miss Tracy. "So the Earth is revolving around the sun and rotating at the same time. You may not know this, but the Earth is also tilted to the side a little. Emily, can you tilt to the side?"

"I think I'm going to—" said Emily.

She never had the chance to finish her

sentence. Because that's when the weird-est thing in the history of the world happened.

Emily fell down.

And then she threw up.

It was gross!

I don't think that happens with real planets.

Throwing Up and Throwing Down

Mr. Cooper rushed over to the intercom and called the front office.

"One of my students just threw up!" he shouted into the phone.

A few seconds later there was a weird noise outside our classroom door. It sounded like a lawn mower was coming down the hallway.

But it wasn't a lawn mower. It was Miss Lazar, our school custodian! She was riding her motorized scooter. Miss Lazar was wearing her big blue overalls with the letters *SC* on the front.

"Have no fear! It is I, Super Custodian!"

said Miss Lazar as she hopped off the scooter. "What happened?"

"Emily got sick," Ryan said, pointing at Emily on the floor.

"This looks like a job for Super Custodian!" said Miss Lazar. "Any time finger paint is spilled, or somebody loses their retainer in the garbage can, or a child throws up, Super Custodian will be at your service to—"

"Can you just clean up the mess, please?" asked Mr. Cooper.

"You can count on me!" Miss Lazar said. She put on a pair of big yellow plastic gloves. "I'll have this cleaned up in a jiffy."

"I'm sorry I made a mess," Emily said.

"No worries," said Miss Lazar. "I love messes! If kids didn't make messes, I wouldn't have a job. So make all the messes you want. In fact, I wish you kids would throw up more. I don't have enough work to do."

Miss Lazar is bizarre.*

Suddenly Mrs. Cooney, our school nurse, came running in.

"Emily, are you okay?" asked Mrs. Cooney as she put a cold rag on Emily's forehead.

"I think so," said Emily.

While Mrs. Cooney was taking care of

---

*A footnote is a note that's on your foot. Any dumbhead knows that. But why would you put notes on your feet?

Emily and Miss Lazar was cleaning up the mess, Miss Tracy got all excited.

"This is what I call a teachable moment!" she said. "Emily didn't really throw up, did she? No, she threw down."

WHAT?!

"You just demonstrated the law of gravity, Emily," Miss Tracy told her. "Did any of you kids ever hear of Sir Isaac Newton?"

"Is he the guy who invented Fig Newtons?" I asked.

"Not exactly," replied Miss Tracy. "Isaac Newton is one of the most famous scientists in history. He discovered gravity. Who can tell us what gravity is?"

Smarty-pants Andrea had already

looked it up on her smartphone. She read off her screen, "Gravity is the force of attraction by which objects tend to fall toward the center of the Earth."

"HUH?" we all said, which is also "HUH" backward.

"Let me explain it another way," said Miss Tracy. "I'm going to tell you a little story. It was the year 1666. Isaac Newton was twenty-three years old, and he was sitting under a tree in his mother's garden in England. Suddenly an apple fell off the tree and hit him on the head."

That was a weird story.

"Newton noticed that the apple fell straight down," Miss Tracy continued. "It didn't fall sideways. It didn't fall up. So he came to the conclusion that all objects are drawn toward the Earth's center by a force called gravity. Gravity is what makes things fall down."

WHAT? That made no sense at all. Where else is an apple gonna fall but down? Somebody had to discover that

stuff falls down instead of up? That's a discovery? Everybody knows stuff falls down! I could have told Miss Tracy that, and I'm just in third grade.

That Fig Newton guy was weird. And Miss Tracy is spacey.

"Let's try an experiment," said Miss Tracy as she picked up a coffee mug from Mr. Cooper's desk and held it up in the air. "What do you think will happen if I let go of this coffee mug?"

"It will fall down," shouted Michael.

"Let's do the experiment and find out," said Miss Tracy.

"Wait! Don't!" shouted Mr. Cooper.

It was too late. Miss Tracy let go of the

coffee mug. It fell down and broke into a million hundred pieces on the floor.

"Oh, snap!" yelled Ryan.

"See?" said Miss Tracy. "That's gravity at work!"

"You broke my lucky coffee mug!" shouted Mr. Cooper.

"Don't worry," said Miss Lazar. "I'll clean that mess up as soon as I finish with this mess. I love cleaning up messes."

"Just as gravity made Emily fall down and throw down, it's also the force that holds our solar system together," said Miss Tracy. "The sun's gravity holds the Earth in its orbit. The Earth's gravity holds the moon in its orbit."

That gravity stuff was pretty cool, but I wasn't thinking about gravity at that moment. I was thinking about Mr. Cooper. He looked mad.

Grown-Ups Behaving Badly

Mr. Cooper is a pretty easygoing guy, but he wasn't happy when Miss Tracy prevented him from doing his math lesson. And after Miss Tracy broke his lucky coffee mug, he looked *really* angry. If he had been in a cartoon, smoke would have been pouring out of his ears.

"Well, I must be going," said Miss Tracy. "I've got to talk to the other classes about astronomy."

"Wait!" said Mr. Cooper. "Before you go, can I ask you a question about gravity?"

"Of course," said Miss Tracy.

"Let's say the sun's gravity pulled a planet closer," said Mr. Cooper. "What would happen?"

"It would get very hot on that planet," Miss Tracy replied. "It might even burn up."

"Do you mean like this?" asked Mr. Cooper.

And with that, he took a little lighter out of his pocket. Then he grabbed Miss

Tracy's hat with all the balls hanging from it. Then he flicked his lighter and a little flame appeared.

"No! Don't!" shouted Miss Tracy.

That's when the weirdest thing in the history of the world happened.

Mr. Cooper held the lighter under one of the Ping-Pong balls!

The Ping-Pong ball ignited!

And then the whole hat went up in flames!

"Oh, snap!" said Ryan. "Mr. Cooper set Miss Tracy's hat on fire!"

Mr. Cooper threw the hat on the floor and stomped all over it to put the fire out. Miss Tracy's hat was totally ruined.

It was hilarious. And we got to see it with our own eyes!

Well, it would be pretty hard to see something with somebody else's eyes.

Now it was Miss Tracy who was all upset.

"That was my favorite hat!" she yelled. "I can't believe you set it on fire!"

"You broke my coffee mug!" Mr. Cooper shouted back at her.

"I was trying to teach the children about gravity," yelled Miss Tracy. "It was just a mug."

"It was my lucky mug!" shouted Mr. Cooper.

"Oh, stop being a baby!"

"You're the baby!

"No, you are!"

"No, you are!"

They went back and forth like that for a while. Then Miss Tracy stormed out of the room. But a second later she came marching back. She looked really angry.

"I forgot to tell you kids about meteors,"

she said as she picked up an eraser from the whiteboard. "A meteor is a piece of rock that falls from outer space into the Earth's atmosphere. It can cause a lot of damage. Pretend that Mr. Cooper is the Earth and this eraser is a meteor."

And you'll never believe what she did next. She reared back and threw the eraser at Mr. Cooper!

It looked like it was going to hit him in the head!

He ducked!

The eraser hit a plant on the windowsill and knocked it over.

"Oh, snap!" said Ryan. "Miss Tracy threw an eraser at Mr. Cooper!"

"I can't believe you did that!" shouted
Mr. Cooper.

"You set my hat on fire!"

"You broke my lucky mug!"

Wow! It was amazing! They were yelling
at each other like a couple of bratty kids. I

hadn't seen grown-ups act so immaturely since last week when my mother asked my father to take out the garbage.

"I don't like to see all this violence," said Andrea. "I believe it sets a bad example for children."

"What do you have against violins?" I asked Andrea.

"Not violins, Arlo! Violence!"

It didn't matter if Andrea liked violins or not. Because after that, things got even weirder. Mr. Cooper was *really* mad.

He grabbed Miss Tracy!

They started wrestling with each other!

Mr. Cooper picked up Miss Tracy!

He held her over his head!

Then he started spinning around!

"If a planet spins too fast," he yelled, "the centrifugal force could make it fly out of its orbit."

"Oh, snap!" said Ryan. "I think Mr. Cooper is gonna throw Miss Tracy out the window!"

I bet he would have, too. But you'll never believe who walked into the door at that moment.

Nobody! It would hurt if you walked into a door. I thought we went over that in Chapter One. But you'll never believe who walked into the doorway.

It was Mr. Klutz!

"I just wanted to see how everybody

was making out," he said. "Whoa! What's going on in here?"

Mr. Cooper put Miss Tracy down.

"Nobody's making out," said Michael. "The teachers were fighting."

"We weren't fighting!" said Mr. Cooper.

"That's right," said Miss Tracy. "Mr. Cooper and I were just teaching the students about astronomy."

It sure looked like a fight to me.

"What's that burning smell?" asked Mr. Klutz.

"Mr. Cooper set Miss Tracy's hat on fire," said Andrea.

"She started it!" shouted Mr. Cooper.

"I did not!" yelled Miss Tracy.

It looked like they were going to start fighting again, but Mr. Klutz stepped between them.

"Stop this right now!" he hollered. "It doesn't matter who started it! Miss Tracy! I'm so disappointed. You were supposed to help the students get more engaged."

"Ugh, gross!" I said. "We're too young to get engaged!"

"Both of you, go to my office!" shouted Mr. Klutz. "And think about what you did."

Mr. Cooper and Miss Tracy hung their heads and shuffled out of the room.

That was weird.

I never knew that astronomy could be so interesting!

The Secret Door

We were all sure that Mr. Cooper and Miss Tracy were going to get fired for fighting. But they weren't. Here's what happened. . . .

Right after dinner that night, my mom told me we had to run an errand.

"Where are we going?" I asked.

"It's a surprise," Mom replied.

So I got in the car and we drove a million hundred miles. And do you know where we ended up?

At Ella Mentry School!

"I have to go to school at *night*?" I asked my mom. "That's not fair!"*

"This is going to be fun, A.J.," my mom told me. "Just go inside."

I got out of the car. It was getting dark out. I climbed the steps to the front door. And guess who was waiting for me?

Miss Tracy and Mr. Cooper! I guess they made up.

"What are you doing here?" I asked.

---

*By the way, just so you know, nothing is fair. That's the first rule of being a kid.

48

"*Shhhh*! Follow us!" they whispered.

Miss Tracy and Mr. Cooper led me down the hall.

"This is a secret door," Mr. Cooper whispered. "Nobody knows about it."

He opened the secret door and we went inside. Then we climbed the secret staircase. It was like we were secret agents. We kept climbing. Then we went through another secret doorway.

And you'll never believe in a million hundred years where the secret doorway led.

To the roof of the school!

Not only that, but my whole class was up there.

I had been on the roof one time before. That was when Andrea got hypnotized by our school counselor, Dr. Brad, and she went crazy. You can read about it in a book called *Dr. Brad Has Gone Mad!*

"What are you all doing up here?" I asked.

"We're going to look at the stars!" said Andrea.

That made sense. I guess Miss Tracy was taking us up on the roof because it's closer to the sky, so we'd have a better view. That's the same reason why your nose gets sunburned when you lie on the beach—because it's closer to the sun than the rest of your face. (I know lots of stuff like that because I'm in the gifted and talented program.)

There were blankets, so we wouldn't have to lie on the roof, which is yucky. I found a spot next to Ryan and Alexia.

"Do you see anything?" asked Miss Tracy.

"I see the sky," said Andrea.

Well, duh. Of course Andrea saw the sky. There was nothing else to see up there. What is Andrea's problem?

"Our eyes have to adjust to the dark," said Miss Tracy. "Isn't it peaceful up here on the roof?"

"Yes," said all the girls.

"No," said all the boys.

Miss Tracy told us about the Milky Way. I always thought it was just a candy bar. But it turns out the Milky Way is the galaxy that our sun and solar system belong to. She said there were a trillion stars in the Milky Way, and a hundred billion planets.

"WOW," we all said, which is "MOM" upside down.

"Is that the Big Dipper?" asked Mr. Cooper, pointing at the sky.

"It certainly is," replied Miss Tracy. She said the Big Dipper is made up of seven stars that form the shape of a dipper.

Huh? What's a dipper? I never heard of a dipper. I didn't see any big dipper up there. I just saw a bunch of stars.

I was going to ask what a dipper was, but I figured everybody else knew what a dipper was, and I didn't want anybody to know I didn't know.

"If we're lucky, we'll get to see a meteor shower," said Miss Tracy. "Does anybody know what that is?"

"That's when a meteor gets dirty, and it has to take a shower," I said. "And then it sprinkles Comet all over itself to clean off."

Ryan and Michael were the only ones who laughed at my joke.

Little Miss Know-It-All was going to tell everybody what a meteor shower was, but she never got the chance, because that's when the most amazing thing in the history of the world happened.

"Look!" said Neil. "A shooting star!"

It was cool watching the shooting star shoot across the sky.

"Actually a shooting star is a piece of rock or even metal that falls from outer space into the Earth's atmosphere," said Miss Tracy.

"I'm scared!" said Emily, who's scared of everything. "What if a shooting star hits our school?"

"Oh, it will burn up long before it could get to Earth, Emily," Miss Tracy assured her. "There's nothing to worry about."

"I'm still scared."

Sheesh, get a grip!

We looked at the stars for a long time. Miss Tracy told us that they were millions of light-years away. That's really far.

Looking at the stars makes you think

about stuff you never thought about before.

"Where do you think the universe ends?" asked Michael.

"It can't go on forever, can it?" asked Ryan.

"Nobody knows," said Neil.

"Do you think there's life out there?" asked Alexia.

"Maybe there's somebody up on a roof on another planet looking at the sky just like we are right now," I said.

"I want to be an astronomer when I grow up," Andrea said.

"Me too," said Emily, who always wants to do whatever Andrea does.

"Isn't the universe amazing?" said Miss Tracy.

After we looked at the sky some more, Miss Tracy showed us something even better: juice and cookies! She had baked cookies in the shapes of the planets.

"I want to eat Mars," said Ryan, who will eat anything, even stuff that isn't food.

"I want to eat Jupiter," I said. "That's the biggest planet, so it will be the biggest cookie."

"Ha-ha!" Andrea shouted, holding a cookie up in the air. "I got Jupiter first, Arlo. You'll have to eat Mercury, the smallest cookie."

I was going to say something mean to

Andrea. But that's when the most amazing thing in the history of the world happened.

I'm not going to tell you what it was.

Okay, okay, I'll tell you.

But you have to read the next chapter.

So nah-nah-nah boo-boo on you!

A Dot in the Sky

While Andrea was holding up the Jupiter cookie, I noticed a tiny dot in the sky. It looked like it was moving.

"Look!" I shouted. "What is *that* thing? A satellite?"

"I don't think so," said Miss Tracy as she picked up a telescope. "And it's not a shooting star either."

"What is it?" asked Ryan.

"I really don't know," admitted Miss Tracy.

Boy, if she didn't know, nobody would know. Miss Tracy knows everything there is to know about astronomy.

The dot in the sky looked like it was getting bigger.

"It's coming closer!" shouted Ryan.

"I hear something too!" said Alexia. "It's like a buzzing sound!"

The dot in the sky kept getting bigger and bigger. It was silver, and there were flames shooting out the back of it.

"I think it's a spaceship!" shouted Neil.

Neil was right. It was a spaceship. And it was coming down right over our heads!

"I'm scared," said Emily.

We were all scared.

"Run for your lives!" shouted Neil.

"No," said Mr. Cooper. "We must be strong."

Everybody huddled together and watched. The spaceship hovered for a few seconds over our heads and then it slowly landed on the other side of the roof.

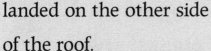

"Maybe they're f-friendly," said Andrea, shivering with fear.

"Or maybe they're going to destroy the Earth," I said.

"*Shhhh*," said Miss Tracy. "Let's all be as quiet as possible."

"I can't look!" whispered Emily.

After about a minute, a hatch opened at the bottom of the spaceship. And you'll never believe in a million hundred years who climbed down the ladder.

It was Mr. Granite, our old teacher!

"Mr. Granite!" we all shouted as we ran over to hug him.

"I missed you!" Mr. Granite said.

"We missed you too!"

It was great to see Mr. Granite again. We hugged for a long time. He said we had all grown up a lot since the last time he saw us.

"Why did you come back to Earth?" I asked him. "Are you going to be a teacher again?"

"No," Mr. Granite replied. "I seem to have forgotten my car keys. Did any of you see them?"

WHAT?!

"No," we all replied.

"Where did you last see your car keys?" asked Andrea.

"If I knew where I last saw them, it would be easy to find them," said Mr. Granite.

"Wait a minute," said Miss Tracy. "You flew millions of light-years back to Earth just because you forgot your car keys?"

"They must be here somewhere," replied Mr. Granite, looking around. "I thought I would be able to find them if I retraced my steps."

"We could look in the lost-and-found box by the front office," suggested Alexia.

"Did you check your pockets?" asked Ryan.

Mr. Granite went through his pockets one by one.

"Oh, wait a minute!" he suddenly shouted. "Here they are! They were in my pocket the whole time! Silly me. Never mind!"

"As long as you're here, are you going to stay on Earth for a while?" asked Neil.

"No, I'm sorry, but I have to go," Mr. Granite said as he climbed the ladder of the spaceship again. "My car is double-parked."

"Good-bye, Mr. Granite!" we all said, waving to him.

"Good-bye!"

The hatch closed. A few seconds later the engine fired up and Mr. Granite's spaceship blasted off.

That was weird.

It's Not Fair!

The next morning at school, Mr. Cooper came flying into the classroom. And I do mean flying. Mr. Cooper thinks he's a superhero. But he's not a very good one, because he bumped into Ryan's desk, tripped over the garbage can, and fell on the floor.

"I'm okay!" he said, jumping to his feet. "Everybody open your math book to page twenty-three."

Ugh, I hate math. I was about to open my math book, but I never got the chance. You'll never believe who poked her head into the door at that moment.

Nobody! Why would anybody want to poke their head into a door? You should know that by now. You really need to work on your reading comprehension.

But you'll never believe who poked her head into the door*way*. It was Miss Tracy! She was holding a bunch of big circles made out of cardboard.

"It is I," she announced, "Miss Universe!"

"Not again," Mr. Cooper grumbled, closing his math book.

"We need to work on our astronomy play," Miss Tracy said.

Oh, yeah, the play. Ugh. We had to put on a play for the whole school to cap off Space Week. The parents were invited to come and everything.

"I thought it would be fun to take the school on a tour of the solar system," Miss Tracy told us. "One of the second-grade classes made these beautiful planets. Each of you can be a different planet."

"Ooooh," I shouted, "I have dibs on planet Earth."

Ha! In Andrea's face! I beat her to it for

once. So nah-nah-nah boo-boo on Andrea.

"I like your enthusiasm, A.J.," said Miss Tracy, "but I don't think we need any of you to be planet Earth. Kids already know a lot about our planet. But who wants to be Saturn? It's such a beautiful planet, with those pretty rings around it."

"I'll be Saturn!" said Andrea, jumping out of her seat. "My mom is always saying that I'm beautiful."

"Okay, Andrea, you can be Saturn," said Miss Tracy, handing Andrea one of the big cardboard circles.

"How come *she* gets to be Saturn?" I shouted. "It's not fair!"

"I'm sorry, A.J.," Miss Tracy told me.

"Andrea asked first. Let me see here. The rings of Saturn need to be attached. A.J., will you please come up here and give Andrea the rings?"

"*Ooooo,*" Ryan said. "A.J. is going to give Andrea a ring! They must be in *love*!"

"It's a wedding ring!" shouted Michael.

If those guys weren't my best friends, I would hate them.

I gave Andrea the rings of Saturn, complaining the whole time that it wasn't fair. Mr. Cooper had been sitting in the back of the room, but he got up and came to the front.

"I'd like to make a suggestion," Mr. Cooper said. "Instead of having the kids fight over which planet they get to be, maybe we should put all their names in a box and pick them randomly. That would make it fair to everyone."

"That's a good idea," said Miss Tracy. "Does everybody agree that would be fair?"

"Yes," we all said.

Mr. Cooper found a cardboard box and put in slips of paper with all our names on them. Then he mixed the names up and handed the box to Miss Tracy.

"Let's start with Mercury, the planet that is closest to the sun," she said, reaching into the box and pulling out a name. "Emily will be Mercury."

"Yay!" shouted Emily.

"Next will be Venus," said Miss Tracy as she reached into the box. "Venus was named after the Roman goddess of love, and she will be . . . Alexia."

"Yay!" shouted Alexia.

Ugh. Miss Tracy said the *L* word. I'm glad she didn't pick *me* to be Venus. The guys would make fun of me for the rest of my life.

"Next comes Mars, which was named after the Roman god of war," said Miss Tracy. "Mars will be played by . . . Michael."

"Boo-yah!" shouted Michael. "Mars kicks butt."

Bummer in the summer! I was hoping that I would be Mars.

"The next planet is the biggest planet, Jupiter," said Miss Tracy. "Jupiter will be . . . Ryan."

"Yay!" shouted Ryan. "I'm the biggest, so that means I'm number one."

"I know a poem about Jupiter," said

Andrea, raising her hand.

"I'd love to hear it," said Miss Tracy.

"Girls go to college to get more knowledge," recited Andrea. "Boys go to Jupiter to get more stupider."

All the girls laughed even though Andrea didn't say anything funny. Miss Tracy went to pick the next name out of the box.

"Next comes Saturn," she said. "And the student who gets Saturn will be . . . Yes, it's Andrea again!"

"Yay!" shouted Andrea.

Ugh. She always gets what she wants. It's not fair.

"Only two planets are left," said Miss

Tracy as she reached into the box. "Neptune is the coldest planet, and it will be played by . . . Neil."

"Yay!" shouted Neil. "I'm the coldest, so that means I'm number one."

"Okay," said Miss Tracy. "I have one student left and one planet left. Last but not least, A.J. will be . . . Uranus."

WHAT?!

Everybody started giggling and elbowing and smirking.

"Oh, snap!" said Ryan. "A.J. is Uranus."

"But I don't *want* to be Uranus," I shouted. "It's not fair!"

"Sure it's fair, A.J.," said Mr. Cooper. "Miss Tracy picked the names randomly."

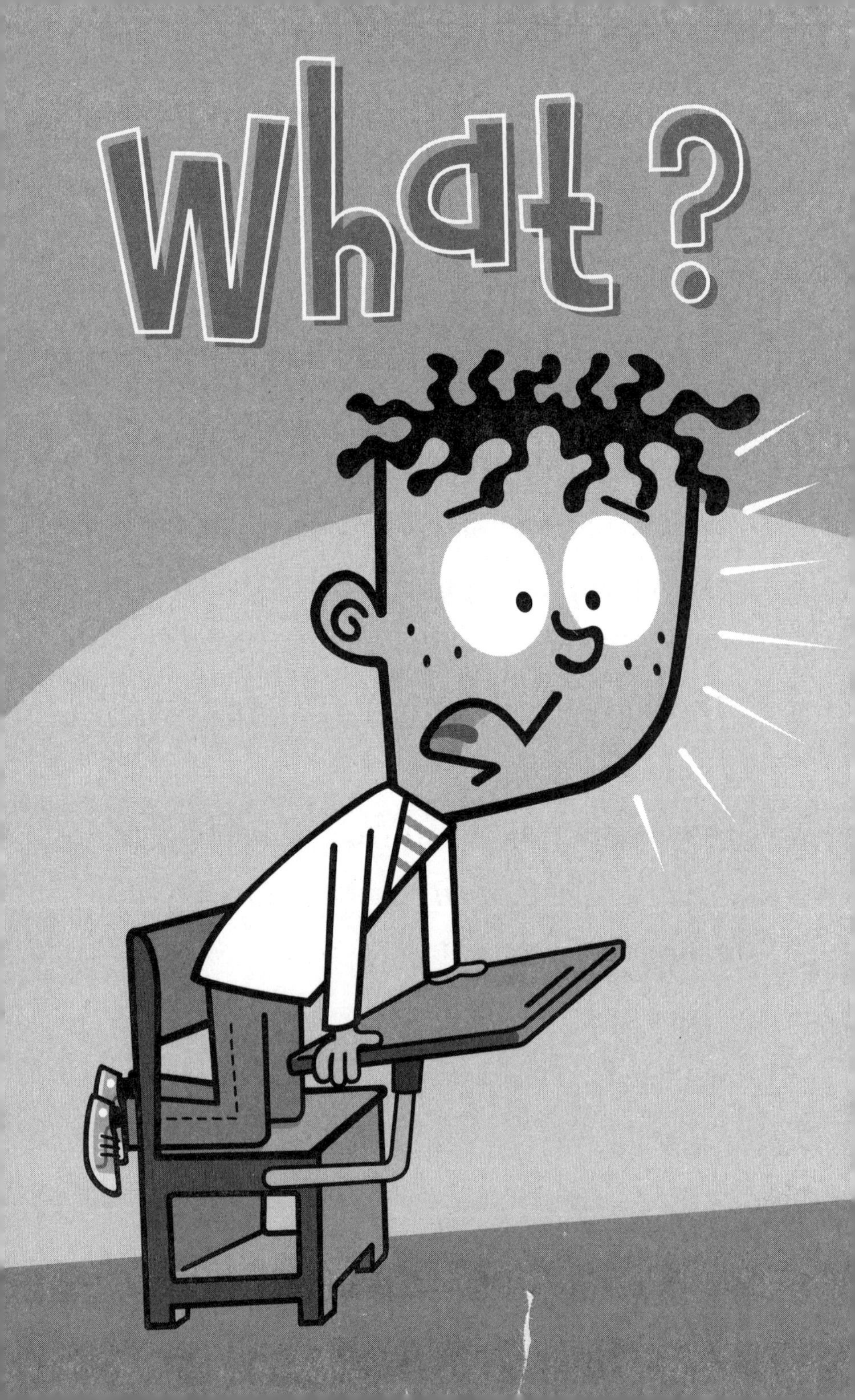
What?

"Uranus is a wonderful planet, A.J.," Miss Tracy told me. "It has twenty-seven known moons."

"Hey, A.J.," said Michael, "I think you should pull your pants down in the middle of the play to show everybody the moons of Uranus!"

Everybody laughed even though Michael didn't say anything funny.

"I don't *want* to be Uranus," I shouted again.

"Well, somebody has to be Uranus," said Miss Tracy. "We can't have a tour of the solar system without Uranus."

"Does anybody want to switch planets with me?" I asked the class.

"No!" everybody replied.

"Hey, Arlo," said Andrea, "maybe you can sing a little song about Uranus."

Then she started singing that song she always sings from *Annie*. But instead of singing the word "tomorrow," she sang "Uranus."

"No!" I shouted. "I'm not singing a song about Uranus! What about Pluto? Why can't I be Pluto?"

"Pluto isn't a planet," said Miss Tracy.

WHAT?!

"My mother told me that Pluto was a planet," I said.

"Pluto *was* a planet," Miss Tracy replied. "But it's not a planet anymore."

Says who? What happened to Pluto? How can something be a planet one day and then the next day it's not a planet anymore?

I wanted to run away to Antarctica and go live with the penguins. Penguins don't have to put on dumb plays and force one of them to be Uranus.

Everybody was laughing at me. The guys would be making fun of me forever. This was the worst day of my life.

It's not fair!

A Tour of the Solar System

Space Week was almost over. The whole school had been involved. Some of the classes made arts and crafts projects about the solar system. Some wrote poems. The fifth graders got to go on a field trip to a planetarium.

My dad dropped me off at school on his way to work. When we pulled into the drop-off line, there was a sign on the front lawn. . . .

COME SEE MISS UNIVERSE TODAY.

"Are you going to see our class play?" I asked him. "It's right after the morning announcements."

"Sorry, A.J.," my dad replied. "I have to get to work. But Mom will be there for sure."

After the morning announcements, we walked a million hundred miles to the all-purpose room. I don't know why they call it the all-purpose room. You can't go kayaking in there.*

Anyway, everybody from kindergarten

---

*Sometimes we call it the all-porpoise room, even though there are no dolphins in there.

up to fifth grade was in the all-purpose room. There was a special section for parents in the back, and it was filled with moms. There were no dads at all.

Everybody was buzzing. But not really, because we're people and not bees. Mr. Klutz climbed up on the stage and made a peace sign with his fingers, which means "shut up."

"Welcome, everyone," announced Mr. Klutz. "Blah blah blah blah. Space Week has been amazing. Blah blah blah blah. We learned a lot about astronomy. Blah blah blah blah. And we couldn't have done it without Miss Tracy. Or as we like to call her, Miss Universe."

Miss Tracy climbed up on the stage, and

everybody gave her a round of applause. That's when you clap your hands in a big circle.

"Thank you," Miss Tracy said, taking a bow. "I've had a wonderful time with the students of Ella Mentry School. Blah blah blah blah. It would take a very long time to do a real tour of the solar system, but Mr. Cooper's third-grade class would like to take you on a simulated tour."

We lined up on the stage with our cardboard planets. The lights dimmed. Weird music started playing. Emily stepped forward, and a spotlight shined on her.

"I am Mercury," Emily said. "I'm the smallest planet. My surface is wrinkled, and I have almost no atmosphere. But I have the most craters, because I've been hit by lots of asteroids and comets."

Everybody gave Emily a round of applause. Then Alexia stepped forward.

"I am Venus," Alexia said. "I'm the hottest planet. It can reach 471 degrees Celsius on me. A day on Venus lasts longer than a year on Venus because I rotate very slowly."

Everybody gave Alexia a round of applause as she turned around. Michael stepped forward.

"I am Mars," Michael said. "They call me the red planet. If you lived on me, you could jump three times higher because I have less gravity than Earth. And I have the tallest mountain in the solar system."

Michael got a round of applause. Ryan stepped forward.

"I am Jupiter," said Ryan. "I'm more than twice as large as all the other planets put together. There's a storm on me that's been going on for 350 years! I wish it would stop already!"

More applause and a few laughs. Andrea stepped forward.

"I am Saturn," Andrea said. "Aren't my rings pretty? They're made of chunks of ice and dust and rock. Oh, and I also have fifty-three moons."

Applause. Neil stepped forward.

"I am Neptune," said Neil. "I'm the far-thest planet from the sun, almost three billion miles away. I'm blue too, and that's why I was named after the Roman god of the sea."

Applause. I stepped forward.

"I am Uranus," I said.

That's when the giggling started in the all-purpose room.

"It's very hard to see Uranus."

More giggling.

"You can see Uranus with your naked eye, but you can see it a lot better with a telescope."

As soon as I said "naked," all the guys started giggling.

"Uranus is tilted, so it's almost on its side."

More giggling.

"Most people don't know this, but there are rings around Uranus."

Everybody in the audience was giggling. Even some of the parents were laughing at me. That's it! I decided that I had enough.

"Hey, knock it off!" I shouted. "I didn't want to be Uranus! I wanted to be Saturn! You think I like this? It's not my fault they named the planet Uranus! Laugh all you want. I'm going to keep saying it. Uranus! Uranus! Uranus!"

Everybody stopped laughing. Nobody said a word. There was total silence in the

all-purpose room. You could hear a pin drop in there.* Everybody was looking at me.

I didn't know what to say. I didn't know what to do. I had to think fast. So I did the only thing I could do. I started singing that song Andrea made up.

"Uranus! Uranus! I love ya, Uranus," I sang. "You're always a day away."

All the kids in my class joined in. The next thing I knew, everybody in the all-purpose room was singing the Uranus song! And when it was done, the audience gave me a standing ovation.

---

*Well, that is if anybody brought pins to the all-purpose room with them.

Miss Tracy came over to me. She put a crown on my head and a sash around my neck. It said MR. UNIVERSE on it. Everybody went crazy.

I thought that was the end of it, but you'll never believe what happened next.

"We have a special guest with us today," said Miss Tracy. "I'd like to introduce the *real* Miss Universe. . . ."

That's when another lady came out on the stage. She was pretty and smiling, and she was wearing a bathing suit.

"Hi, everybody!" said the real Miss Universe as she waved her hand.

All the moms rushed forward to take pictures of the real Miss Universe.

"My husband will love this!" one of the moms said.

"How about a picture of Miss Universe and Mr. Universe together?" suggested Mr. Klutz.

"Sure!" said the real Miss Universe. And then she put her arm around me while everybody took pictures. It was the greatest day of my life.

"Hey, how come A.J. gets to be Mr. Universe?" shouted Ryan. "I want to be Mr. Universe!"

"It's not fair!" said Michael and Neil.

Nah-nah-nah boo-boo on them.

The Ending . . . of the World

Everybody was buzzing about the real Miss Universe, so Mr. Klutz had to make the shut-up peace sign to make people stop talking.

"Wasn't Space Week fun?" asked Mr. Klutz. "I think we all learned a lot about astronomy. Before we dismiss everyone, does anybody have any questions for Miss Tracy?"

A bunch of hands went up. Miss Tracy called on one of the fourth graders.

"How fast does the Earth turn around?" asked a girl.

"Good question!" said Miss Tracy. "The Earth spins at about a thousand miles an hour."

WHAT?! That's way faster than the speed limit.

"I'm scared," said Emily. "I think I feel dizzy."

Oh no, not again.

"Don't worry," said Miss Tracy. "The Earth will gradually slow down when the sun dies out."

WHAT?!

"Excuse me," said the real Miss Universe. "Did you just say that the sun is going to die out?"

"Yes, of course," Miss Tracy replied. "In five billion years, the core of the sun will run out of hydrogen and become less bright. Then the Earth and all the planets in the solar system will disintegrate."

"The sun is going to . . . die?" asked Alexia.

"What does 'disintegrate' mean?" asked Ryan.

Andrea had already looked it up on her smartphone.

"Disintegrate means 'to break apart into many small pieces'!" she shouted.

"The sun is gonna die!" shouted Michael. "The Earth is gonna break apart! Miss Tracy said so!"

"Yes, but it won't be for five billion years," said Miss Tracy.

"That's like tomorrow!" I shouted.

"There's nothing to worry about," said Miss Tracy. "We'll all be dead—"

"We'll all be dead!" shouted one of

the fourth graders.

"Help!" somebody hollered. "The world is going to end!"

"Run for your lives!" shouted Neil.

"We've got to do something!" shouted Emily.

Everybody started yelling and screaming and shrieking and hooting and hollering. You should have been there!

"Students! Calm down!" shouted Mr. Klutz.

It was no use. Everybody started running around and bumping into one another trying to get to the emergency exits. Even the moms and teachers were freaking out. Somebody banged into the real Miss Universe, and she fell off the stage.

Well, that's pretty much what happened during Space Week. Maybe the real Miss Universe will come back when our dads are there. Maybe we'll get to page twenty-three in our math books. Maybe Mr. Granite will lose his car keys again. Maybe

Emily will demonstrate the law of gravity again by throwing up. Maybe Isaac Newton will eat some Fig Newtons. Maybe Mr. Cooper will throw Miss Tracy out the window. Maybe Andrea will start to like violins. Maybe I'll find out what a dipper is. Maybe Pluto will become a planet again. Maybe we'll figure out a way to stop the sun from dying and the Earth from breaking apart.

But it won't be easy!

DON'T MISS THESE BOOKS BY
DAN GUTMAN!